Stinkified

A book about farts

By L. M. Dunn

<u>Science Fiction</u>
Intergalactic Justice Council

<u>Thriller</u>
Wasted Time

<u>Travel</u>
Skagway: Alaska's Little Nugget

For all you gasbags

Special thanks to my cover models
Lois
&
Steve

Stinkified
A book about farts

L. M. Dunn

Photography by
L. M. Dunn

Rudimentary Illustrations by
L. M. Dunn

Follow at
@LMDunn888

A fart is one of those natural bodily functions that evokes satisfaction, surprise, laughter, disgust, anger and even horror. We all do it. As a matter of fact, I just let a nice one out of the chute while I'm sitting here. I'm sure there'll be many more where it came from; especially since studies have shown that the average person farts 12 to 25 times a day, expelling .6 to 1.8 liters of gas. I know a few gasbags that are at the high end of the fart spectrum. No doubt a lot of you reading this are acquainted with a few higher end gasbags yourself. You might be one of them. You know who you are. So do your family and friends.

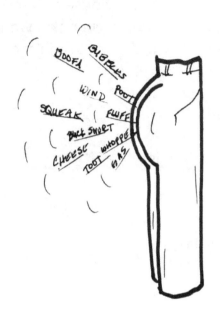

The Word:

The dictionary (online) defines the word fart as, "to expel a flatus (flatus=flate-us) through the anus." The word, itself, stirs up all kinds of emotions and expressions. Kids say the word and giggles follow. When a parent hears their child say the word, they often respond with, "don't say that word, say (such-and-such)." How many of you have a grandma that finds the word to be vulgar? "Don't say that. That's not nice." Been there. We didn't say fart in my house either. We always said "put". Still do. Before starting this book, I went online and asked my friends what word was used in their home growing up.

Here's the result:

Toot	Bubbles
Gas	Cheese
Wind	Fluff
Boofa	Whopper
Buck snort	Poot
Squeak	

Gas:

As you know, farts are gas coming from your insides. But, did you know that this gas comes from either swallowed air or colonic bacteria? Me neither. From swallowed air you get oxygen, nitrogen and carbon dioxide. From bacteria, hydrogen and methane. Somebody decided to analyze this stuff and they found out that intestinal gas is mostly swallowed air. Huh.

Fart Bit:

Less than 1% of gas has a smell. But intestinal bacteria generates compounds containing sulfur. And, according to the GI Society, our noses can detect hydrogen sulfide in concentrations as low as 1/2 part per billion. Wow!
So, you're not gonna get away with it. Somebody will smell it.

To Clench or Not To Clench:

You've all been in a crowded room, at the checkout stand or someplace where you didn't think you could let 'er rip. So, you clench your sphincter and pray for the door to open or the line to move faster all the while building up more and more gas in your belly. Now you're even more bloated. Pain and discomfort ensue. Ugh. Hurry up!

Fart Bit:

Farting is a natural process that releases by-products of the gastrointestinal system, waste. Holding it in can put pressure on the lower intestinal system and cause bloating. A clenched fart may lead to gases being reabsorbed into the body.

Fart Suggestion:

   Find a space, turn your backside away from people and let it rip. You might want to fan your tush before moving away. It might follow you. Or, when the crowd starts moving, let it out as you're walking along. There's too many people to know where it came from.

Fart Bit:

   It's always a good idea to stand when farting whenever possible. Sitting on a hard surface the fart reverberates, amplifying the sound. However, you could just do a little lean forward or to the side.

The Release:
   The act of--

            Farting
            Cutting the cheese
            Passing gas
            Breaking wind
            Crop dusting
            Letting 'er rip.

Is a fart is just a fart? I think not. If you listen carefully, you'll hear the differences. Let me enlighten you to an assortment of gaseous emissions exiting the body via the sphincter.

Fart Bit--

For some, farting is a fetish. It is called eproctophilia. Someone with this fetish is sexually aroused by farting.

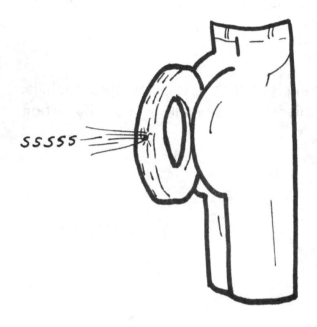

sssss

The Leaky Tire--

   You're super relaxed, laying on the sofa and there it goes--sssss. The sound of air being let out of a tire. It's one of those lengthy, satisfying farts.

The Laugh Fart (AKA The Bust-A-Gut)--

Now these farts are almost always involuntary. You don't know they're coming. They just do. And, they come in a variety of explosions just like laughs.

You know when you're taking a drink and someone says something funny, and you do this little snort thing, pushing that liquid up into your sinuses? It's that kind of laugh/fart conjunction. Somebody says something funny out of the blue, you let out a "HA!", simultaneously the pressure of the laugh forces out a short burst of air. This is similar to the Sneeze Fart.

There's also the big-blast-belly-laugh fart. You're in a group , somebody says/does something funny. Everybody's laughing. Pretty soon it's a pandamonium of laughter. You're laughing at him, he's laughing at her, etc. Someone gets a cramp in their side. More laughing. Then it happens, BOOF. For a quick second, everyone stops, looking around to see who did it. The laugh fest begins again.

Most of the time, there's just the one explosive mishap. Occasionally, you get the Fizzler. After the initial blast, there's more laughing, which creates more pressure. It pushes out yet another fart but of lesser intensity. More laughing. More farting, each one less than the previous one. It's a vicious cycle. Until all that's left is a little phfit; it fizzled out.

The Sneeze Fart--

  Just a quick bit about the Sneeze Fart. I mentioned it in the previous fart. People sneeze. They let out a fart. It's funny. But what about multiple sneezers? Some people sneeze in multiples. I often sneeze in twos. So, is a multiple sneezer also a multiple sneeze farter? Hm. Something to ponder, or listen for.

The Flapper--

This tends to happen if you have fleshy cheeks. You are laying on your side when you let the gas flow. It's a fart with some force. One cheek flaps against the other, creating The Flapper. Kinda like a flag flapping in the wind.

The Flying Fart (AKA The Boeing 747)--

   It never fails, you're flyingon an airplane and not long after getting in the air the bubbles start. Oh damn. You're in a flying tube filled with people packed in like sardines. What do you do? Do you hold it? This is a terrible option because the bubbles keep coming. There's nowhere for them to go. You're already uncomfortable from having little to no room to move. Now what? Do you excuse yourself and head to the bathroom for some relief from the bloat? This is a likely option. But depending on the length of the flight, you could be excusing yourself a lot. Plus there's this: Have you excused yourself and made your way to the tiny bathroom only to find that you can't fart? You're belly is full of trapped gas and your body says--nope. You stand there pushing. Nothing. Push on your tummy. Negative. Your only other option is to drop trau, sit on the pot and hope for the best. If not, bummer. Now you make your way back to your seat, feeling like a hot air balloon. As soon as you sit down and buckle up, the gas is ready to go. You've gotta be kidding me, right? *Heavy sigh* You're mind is consumed with your dwindling options. Do continue to hold it? Maybe, but you really don't want to. Do you excuse yourself once again? Probably not, particularly if you're sitting in the window seat. Or, do you plant one in the soft seat, hoping it dissipates without stink-bombing the row behind you? I'll leave that one up to you.

Fart Bit:

   Apparently, there's a specific reason for the 747. The change in air pressure can affect the body's intestinal system. Makes sense. This change messes with your ears, why not your insides too. Not to worry though. You can purchase carbon-lined underwear; they help to filter the odor. Yes, it's real thing. Google it.

The Spit--

   The name, alone, sounds like it could be a gross one. Not really, though. This one is just the tiniest of farts. Hardly worth a mention. However, it does exist. You know when you're at the movie theatre eating popcorn and you get a hull stuck upside down on your tongue. Those little suckers are hard to move. When you finally get it loose, you spit it out with a little "thp". That's the sound of the Spit Fart--thp.

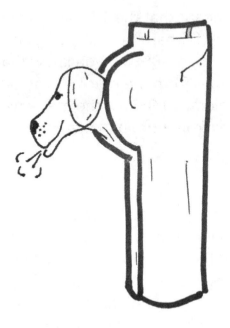

The Whoof--

   This is a half-hearted fart. Not much effort to it. Barely noticeable. Like when your dog hears something but is too lazy to give it a full-on bark. He blows a puff of air out his jowls into a whoof. It sounds like he's barking under his breath. This is the Whoof Fart.

Fart Bit--

   You may have heard that the 1.5 billion cows on the planet have been blamed for harming the environment through methane gas emissions. But did you know that only 5-10% of the methane comes from the rear? It's the other end that is causing the problem. 90-95% of the methane gas released from cows comes from burping.

The Fake-Out--

   It's about time for your "daily constitutional". You know the poop has moved into the chute. So, you grab a magazine, or puzzle book, and head to the toilet. You cop a squat on the pot, making yourself comfortable. Everything relaxes and before you can read the first paragraph, or clue,--phft! That's it. Nothing else. You've been faked-out by a fart. Damn.

The Ploomph--

   If you have ever taken a bath, you have farted in the tub. The release of air against the tub into the bath water elicits a-- ploomph! Instead of dispersing in the water, the air forms bubbles. Those bubbles make their way to the surface. Bam! Instant stinkified air. Like Eddie Murphy says, "You can smell it."

Fart Bit:

You many have noticed that the stink is stronger in the tub, or the shower. You're in a small, enclosed space, so the blast doesn't dissipate as readily. Also, when taking a bath, there's water vapor in the air. Research shows that water vapor enhances your sense of smell. Lucky you.

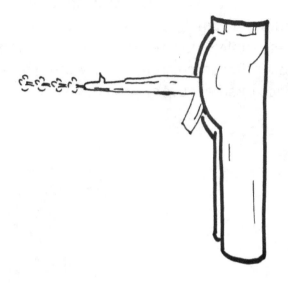

The Ratta-Tatter (AKA The Machine Gun Kelly)--

   Imagine the sound of a machine gun--bap bap bap bap bap. With the Ratta-Tatter, you get a rapid-fire volley of short, snappy farts.

The Juicy Fart--

This is that juicy sounding fart that makes you stop dead in your tracks with that bug-eyed OMG look on your face. It's the "better-go-check-your-panties" fart. Most of the time everything is fine. I don't know why it has that juicy sound. Maybe it's a hot day and there's sweat between your cheeks.

Fart Bit--

Farts are a hot topic in literature, dating back to the ancient Sumerians. You can find fart jokes in the works of Chaucer, Swift, Shakespeare and even Twain.

The Snort--

This fart sounds like a bull that is annoyed. Have you ever been near a bull that's annoyed, or seen a bull-fight on TV? The bull paws the ground and lets out a snort before charging. That sound is the Snort Fart. Some people call it the Buck Snort.

The Snapper--

No, this is not a fishy fart. This is that quick release air between the cheeks fart. You get that nice, crisp--SNAP!

Fart Bit--

Around the turn of the 20th century, a man named Joseph Pujol found fame as a flatulist, professional farter. He was a headliner at the famous Moulin Rouge.

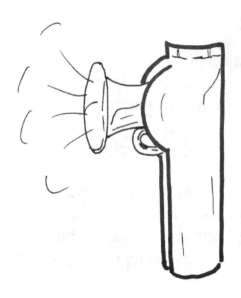

The Tuba--

This one is almost musical. It has that marching band tuba sound--boofa. At home, when someone lets out the Tuba fart, we call them a "Tuba Butt".

The Night Fart(s)--

   You may not know this because you're sleeping, but you release intestinal air at night. Your body is relaxed. All that trapped air now has an avenue without resistance, so out it seeps.
   Your partner is likely very aware of this, especially if you're gassing him/her out. If he/she hasn't mentioned to you that you fart at night, you might want to have the "fart talk", or not. It might be good for a laugh, though.

The Hot Fart (AKA: The Dragon's Breath)--

Every now and then, the dragon breathes fire out of your blow hole. Some of you may be hot farting a lot more than others, depending on what's going in the other end. If you're eating spicy food, chances are you experiencing the Hot Fart. What goes in hot frequently comes out hot.

Fart Bit:

Besides eating spicy foods, hot farts can be the result of little pressure behind the burst. The flatus being released is going to be body temperature, or close to it. A forceful fart is going to pass the air through the cheeks and disperse quicker than a fart that nonchalantly makes its way to the outside, which has that hot sensation. Check it out. The next time you get that heat from your tush, pay attention to the boost behind it.

The Detour--

This one sounds a tad strange. "How does a fart take a detour?", you may be asking. Well here's a scenario for you:

You're sitting on hard surface, a park bench perhaps, and you're wearing tight pants. Even if you don't have tight pants on this can still happen. When you sit, things spread out and clothing gets tighter. Here comes the gas. You know it's coming but you choose not lean to give it some room, instead you let it ride. Maybe there's some people around and you don't want to be obvious.

Because of the conditions you have created, the fart gets caught between you and your clothing. One would think that the gas would just--go away, but it doesn't. A hot bubble has formed in your pants and is seeking the path of least resistance. It has no choice but to detour down your crack, over the taint and up the front, glancing off either the sack or the lips. Your groin is filled with heat, but not in a good way. It's a little icky, almost intrusive like you've been violated by your own--gas. Hopefully, you're not sitting in the park having lunch because once the bubble passes, you're gonna get nice big whiff--of you.

The Sneaky Pete (AKA: The Silent But Deadly)--

This fart here is one of the worst farts known to man (and woman). The reason being, there is no warning system in place. It sneaks between the cheeks without making a sound. Only the gasbag freeing the Sneaky Pete knows of its existence. The people in the near vicinity have no chance of escape. By the time the liberation of the gas is finished, the damage is already been done; eyes are watered and nose hairs are singed.

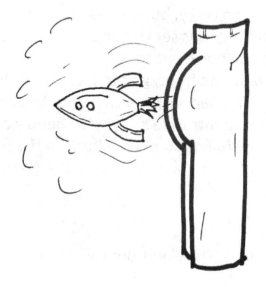

The Rocket--

  This thing is jet-propelled down the chute, through the cheeks and out into the atmosphere like only NASA could formulate. This full-force, top-velocity fart has such pressure that it rattles the anal tissue on the way out, causing the deliverer to flinch at the pain. Youch! That tissue back there is delicate, man.

Fart Bit--

A fart by any other name is still a fart. Here are some other languages and their word for fart:

German	furz
Hawaiian	ala
Norwegian	promp
Croatian	pranuti
Korean	bang-gwi
Malay	kentut
Swedish	fisa
Ukranian	perdity
Spanish	pedo

The Put--

It's that simple little fart that is released without much fanfare. It doesn't have a lot of gusto. Much of the time it goes unnoticed. It's a mundane, small fart; no harm, but some foul.

The Copy Cat--

The Copy Cat is sometimes linked to the Laugh Fart. A group of people, somebody farts, lots of laughing; then, it happens-- a copy cat. The guy next to you rips one because he's laughing so hard, which then continues the laughter. This could potentially go on and on in a contagious fashion. Copy cat after copy cat.

The Toilet Fart (And, The Urinal Fart)--

The Urinal Fart is somewhat different from the Toilet Fart, mostly in the way it plays out. Though, both are related in that they have to do with muscle relaxation when you pee.

For a man standing at a urinal, there is often a release of flatus because he's letting it all go. You can catch your guy doing this in the morning with the first pee of the day.

For a Woman, though, The Toilet Fart can be a very embarrassing experience. It's one thing to expel this fart in the privacy of your own home and whole other thing to do it in a public restroom. So, you go into a stall, prepare the toilet liner, drop trau and have a seat. Then before the pee stream hits the water--TOOMPH! Out comes the Toilet Fart. The thump of the fart bounces of the sides of the bowl, making the perfect little resonance chamber. The acoustics of the tiled restroom enables everyone present to hear it. Oh the horror.

One other note about this fart, as soon as the fart is discharged the person discharging the fart instantly internally gasps and clenches her sphincter in a futile attempt to stop the expulsion. She finishes her business then waits for everyone to leave before exiting the stall.

The Forced Fart--

You all have that one friend that forces a fart. He thinks he's funny. You can certainly tell it's the Forced Fart by the sound. You can see it too. Like when a baby suddenly spaces out kinda like he's really focused on something. The baby's face turns red a makes little baby grunts. It becomes obvious that he's pushing something out. That's what the Forced Fart guy, or gal; looks like a pooping baby.

The Fully-Loaded (AKA: The Oopsy, AKA: The Ruh Roh AKA: The Run to the Bathroom to Shower Off)--

Need I say more?...Yes. I must. This is the one that we're all afraid of; the one that provides maximum gross. Embarrassment too. This is the one that makes you rethink when, where and how you let go of what's boiling up inside you. It makes you afraid to pull the trigger on the next bubble that makes its way down the channel. So if you're already prairie-doggin' it, don't let that sucker go. Squeeze tight, or you'll be in for a hot, sticky mess.

And, bringing up the rear...

The Combo Fart--

   As you've been reading this, you might think that some of the farts you've experience are more than one type of fart at the same time. These are the Combo Farts.
   For example:

   The Hot, Leaky Tire Fart
   The Flapper, Sneeze Fart
   The Juicy, Machine Gun Kelly, Expanding
Cloud, Immanent Dump Fart

   Oh, the odious possibilities.

Put The Stank On Ya'!

   No fart book would be complete without talking about the stink. You already know that the smell comes from sulfurous compounds created in the digestive tract. That's what the professionals say. I say, sometimes it smells like something else is going on.

   But first...

The Cloud--

Everyone has experience The Cloud--and gagged because of it. The gaseous emission that has passed through your buttocks and into the atmosphere--that is The Cloud. When it has yet to be dispersed, it is hot, thick and heavy in the air. The local weatherman could pick this cloud up on his Doppler radar.

As if that's not enough, there's...

The Expanding Cloud--

This is your worst nightmare--being on the receiving end.
You're in a crowd of people, someone lets out a Hot, Sneaky Pete right as you're beginning to inhale. It immediately stops the intake. You get that scrunched up ick-face look. Breathing is not an option; what little air you have in your lungs is full of

stink. It's in your throat--Ack! You taste it on the back of your tongue--Uck! At this point, your choices are few. You hear your heart pounding in your ears. A fresh breath is a must. Soon! You have to move.

Moving a few steps away from the cloud in search of fart-free air, you think you're at a safe enough distance. Tragically, your movement whooshes the ever expanding cloud toward you, unbeknownst to you. Believing you are safe, you exhale the rancid air from your lungs and follow it with a much needed inhale. No! This can't be happening. You haven't moved far enough away. You stop the breath part way--again.

Panic mode sets in. You're mind is reeling. It's a race against time. You're now concerned about toxic fart syndrome. What do you do? Do you keep moving, or do you suck it up and deal with it? Just go ahead and breath in the stink cloud. It'll go away eventually and you'll only be mildly traumatized for a little while. You can handle it, right?

You gotta make a choice. Stay or go? Go! Move, and move quickly. You have to get to that safe distance, whatever that may be. Your lungs are screaming at you. Go, man! Trot it out. Trot. It. Out.

Who cares what it looks like. Everyone else already thinks you did it and you made it worse by moving around. Breathe! Take that deep breath you've been near-dying for. Then another, and another. Make sure you get all that nastiness out of your lungs.

Whew! All is right with the world again. Unfortunately, you have to take this melodramatically harrowing experience with you for the rest of the day. But-you go with the knowledge of what to do if you again find yourself trapped in the Expanding Cloud...

Trot. It. Out.

Back To The Stink...

I know that the odor comes from sulfur compounds created in the body--blah blah blah. Light a match, that smells like sulfur. My nose tells me there's gotta be something else going on. There's some nasty, vile, putrid stuff coming out of people these days.

Fart Bit--

President Gerald Ford blamed his farts on the Secret Service agents that protected him.

The Rotten Egg--

Eh, no big deal. Your average fart smell. It's that sulfur thing. It smells like rotten eggs. Unless you've actually eaten eggs, hard-boiled eggs. They add a whole new element to the Rotten Egg. It adds a meaty component, but not any meat you'd want to eat.

The Imminent Dump--

This one is so dang gross. You know there's a poop in the chute just aching to get out. It's dense hanging in the air. You feel like you're inhaling fecal material.

I don't know how many times I've been at the gym in the morning and been subjected to the Imminent Dump. Ack! It always happens when I'm doing cardio. I'm exercising. I'm breathing heavy. I can't hold my breath on the treadmill, people. It's obvious to me that, at any moment, this person is going to have a poo-mergency. No way am I moving from my treadmill. I've already put in 7 minutes and 48 seconds. Instead, I fan the stench from my nose with my hand, hoping this individual will take notice. All I can think is, "Go sit on the pot, would ya'."

The Old and Dusty--

No offense to old folks but they have a smell unto themselves. It's kinda like walking into a thrift store or an antique store. It's not horrible but it makes your nose crinkle. There's a stuffiness to it. Like when you're stuck in a car with a bunch of people and they're sucking up all the air. It gets so stuffy that you need to put down the window so you can breathe. Like that.

The What The Hell Crawled Up Inside You And Died?--

  This is the kind of stink that is so bad it makes you want to yak. The gag reflex kicks in violently like the dry heaves. This is the one the that makes your eyes water and choke on your own saliva. The one that will clear a room. This is the one that will make you re-think your relationships. The name says it all. I'm talking total stinkification in the worst possible way.

What Did You Eat?:

  Everyone has something that they ingest that causes flatus to develop. Radishes--yikes. It doesn't take long for them to transform into something wicked. And, fast food. It tastes good but is causes bodily eruptions of volcanic proportions. What makes you fart?

Fart Bit--

  Here's a list of foods that can cause gas:
    Dairy--particularly for those who are lactose intolerant.
    Fruit--they contain fiber, which can produce gas.
    Veggies--the green ones are high in fiber.
    Grains--carbs create gas.
    Beans--we all know about beans and bean farts. They have lots of fiber and protien. Gas gas gas.

Nuts--protein, fat and fiber. The trifecta. Cashews are the worst for gasbags.

Carbonated drinks (except seltzer)--they have high amounts of high fructose corn syrup, or artificial sweetener, depending on your drink choice of soda. Both are harder for the body to break down.

Note from me--

I wrote this book with the intention of providing you with comic relief and to remind you that life isn't always serious. In reading this book, I hope you found yourself reminiscing about those funny and/or embarrassing moments that gave you a chuckle.

Cheers!

Where did I get the idea?

Many years ago when I was in 8th grade, I had a class called Speech & Drama. I remember before the school year started, hoping I would get this class and the best teacher. I was super excited to get both. The class consisted of writing and presenting speeches and skits. My classmates and I were always given a topic to write about, ahead of time, by the teacher. Until one day, the teacher said we had to write a speech and we could write about anything we wanted. She, then, gave us the last ten minutes of class to bounce ideas off each other, where we sat.

The whole class was excited about this turn. In the row where I sat, 4 or 5 of us chatted about the ideas we had for this new assignment. Then, this kid across from me says, "I'm gonna write about farts!" We all laughed, of course. But inside, I was loving this idea and I told him so. "Yeah, that's a great idea." A few minutes passed, kids are deciding on their topics and I'm still thinking about that great idea. So, I asked the kid, "Are you going to write about fart?"

"Nah," he says.

I am overjoyed! "Can I do it?," I asked him.

He said I could and the wheels started turning.

Come speech day and the teacher called my name, I walked to the podium and set my speech down so I could see it. (We didn't have to memorize it.) I commenced. My speech contained the different farts and smells. I used hand gestures to convey my topic fully. Everyone laughed, but it was the teacher that caught my attention. She always sat at the back of the class and graded our speeches. This lady was laughing hysterically. My speech really tickled her.

After giving the speech, I took the paper copy to the teacher for grading. This is how it worked in our class. She quickly wrote my grade on the paper and handed it back to me with a smile.

Walking away, I looked at my grade...

AAA+++

Because of a great teacher that gave us 8th graders free reign to write about whatever we wanted, I am able to write and present this literary work of fun to you.

References

badgut.org

dictionary.com

quora.com

webmd.com

thetimesofindia.com

mentalfloss.com

womenshealthmag.com

mensjournal.com

forbes.com

translate.google.com

theconversation.com